SCRIMSHAW'S HOUSE

CHOPPER MOUNTAINS

Airport

For Alice, with grandmotherly love—M.M.

For Ian, with love—M.C.

Text copyright © 1993 by Margaret Mahy
Illustrations copyright © 1993 by Margaret Chamberlain

Margaret K. McElderry Books
Macmillan Publishing Company
866 Third Avenue
New York, NY 10022

Maxwell Macmillan Canada, Inc.
1200 Eglinton Avenue East
Suite 200
Don Mills, Ontario M3C 3N1

Macmillan Publishing Company is part of the Maxwell Communication Group of Companies.

First United States edition

A Vanessa Hamilton Book
Designed by Mark Foster
First published 1993 by Hamish Hamilton Ltd., London
Printed and bound in China by Imago

10 9 8 7 6 5 4 3 2 1

The text of this book is set in Trump Medieval.
The illustrations are rendered in line and wash.

Library of Congress Catalog Card Number: 93-77331

ISBN 0-689-50595-7

A Busy Day for a Good Grandmother

MARGARET MAHY

Illustrated by
Margaret Chamberlain

Margaret K. McElderry Books
New York

Maxwell Macmillan Canada • Toronto
Maxwell Macmillan International • New York • Oxford • Singapore • Sydney

Mrs. Oberon was quietly cleaning her trail bike at her home in the rugged Hambone Hills. Sitting on the veranda rail, her seven cats waited patiently to be fed.

"Milk in a minute!" said Mrs. Oberon. But at that moment the phone rang. It was her son Scrimshaw. He was in a terrible state.

"Oh, Mother, Mother! Wanda's gone to work, and it's my turn to look after little Sweeney. He's cutting his top teeth, and he's weeping and wailing and carrying on something awful. What he needs is a soothing slice of your cock-a-hoop honey cake."

"Well, give him a slice, then, Scrimshaw," suggested Mrs. Oberon.

"Oh, Mother, we've eaten the cock-a-hoop honey cake you sent last week, and I don't know how to make another," wailed Scrimshaw.

"By a lucky chance I have a freshly baked cock-a-hoop honey cake in my cake tin," said Mrs. Oberon. "I'll bring it over at once."

"Wonderful!" cried Scrimshaw, suddenly sounding much more cheerful. "I'll serenade Sweeney on my electric guitar until you arrive."

Mrs. Oberon put the huge tin full of cock-a-hoop honey cake into her backpack. She also packed a pot of blue borage honey, her skateboard, fifty butcher-bean-and-meat balls (made with homegrown butcher beans), and a batch of healthy—but rather heavy—carrot muffins she had baked before breakfast. The backpack bulged as Mrs. Oberon swung it over her strong shoulders. On with her motorbike helmet! A quick vault over the veranda railing, and Mrs. Oberon landed lightly on her trail bike, revved up, and was off and away.

There had been one or two small avalanches overnight, but the weight of the carrot muffins stopped the trail bike from bouncing about too much. Mrs. Oberon reached the river just where the dangerous Riff-Raff Rapids began.

Leaping off her trail bike she jumped straight over the bank and onto her red racing-raft, tied up below. Rafting in and out of the ragged rocks of the Riff-Raff Rapids, she patted her backpack to make sure the cock-a-hoop honey cake was safe and sound.

Mrs. Oberon swept down the squiggly, wriggly, roundabout river, skillfully pushing herself off shoals and shallows, and cunningly avoiding crosscurrents and whirlpools.

At last she shot triumphantly out of the Riff-Raff Rapids into the Swagwallow Swamp. The red raft was going so fast it skipped halfway across the swamp before slowing down. Alligators immediately began to close in on Mrs. Oberon, smiling and snapping their jaws.

However, she was ready for them. Reaching into her backpack she lightly tossed handfuls of butcher-bean-and-meat balls into the water.

A hideous hurly-burly began. Swagwallow Swamp hissed and seethed as alligators fought desperately for the tasty morsels, beating the water with their powerful tails. They all loved the taste of butcher beans. But butcher beans are remarkably sticky.

The alligators spent the next twenty minutes trying to free their fangs from the butcher beans as Mrs. Oberon poled gracefully in between them, whistling softly to herself.

While this was going on, Scrimshaw was playing the electric guitar, and singing to his poor, teething baby.

"Hush-a-bye, baby, with teeth coming through,
Soon you'll have toothypegs, shining and new.
No snarling, my darling, no hullabaloo!
A cock-a-hoop honey cake's heading for you!"

Meanwhile Mrs. Oberon had landed her red raft beside Swagwallow Airport. Her faithful Piper Cherokee airplane was waiting at the end of the runway. Mrs. Oberon checked the fuel—and filled the muffin ejector (an instrument of her own invention) with carrot muffins. She took off to the north, flying up and over the Chopper Mountains where pointed, pearly peaks seemed to nibble at the blue edge of the sky.

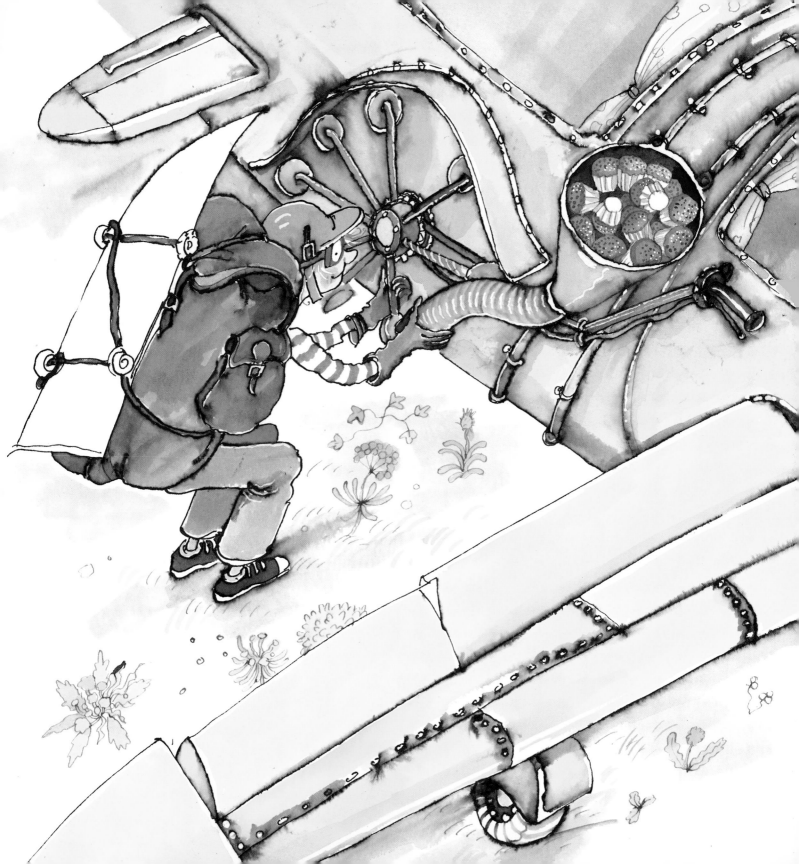

Suddenly, out from a cleft in the mountains soared a sinister swarm of birds.

"Oh, dear! Ice vultures!" muttered Mrs. Oberon. "I was afraid this might happen."

Exceptionally large ice vultures were settling on the wings of the Piper Cherokee, staring hungrily at Mrs. Oberon.

But she released the muffin-ejector control and BOOM! Carrot muffins flew high into the clear mountain air. Off went the vultures, greedily snapping up muffins. And as the muffins were rather heavy (however healthy), the vultures immediately lost altitude. They sank slowly out of sight, flapping their wings madly, while Mrs. Oberon waved to them from her Piper Cherokee and headed for the city airport.

Scrimshaw was desperate. Standing on his head, he played the electric guitar upside down, balancing a bowl of fruit salad on one foot to distract his poor baby. As he did this he sang to Sweeney.

"You've got those teething blues!
Yeah, baby, you've got those teething blues!
The day's going by and there's no good news.
Oh, *wah, wah, waaaaah!*"

But Sweeney howled a *wah, wah, waaaaah* of his own that was even louder than Scrimshaw's.

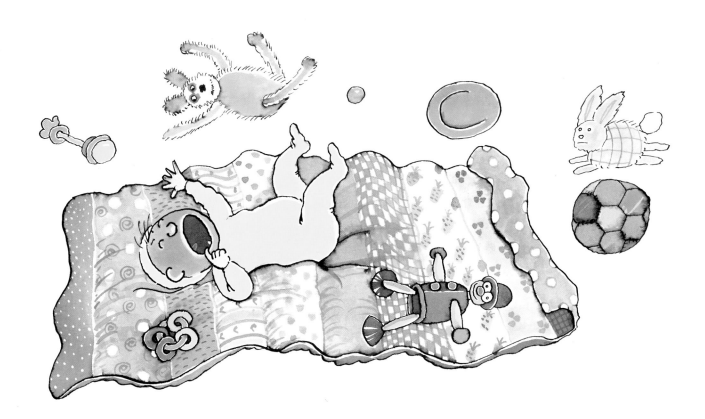

Suddenly, the door burst open. In sailed Mrs. Oberon on her
skateboard, still wearing her motorbike helmet and her backpack.

Whisking the cake tin from her backpack she opened it at once. There, inside, was a great, big, wholesome, healthy, sweet and soothing cock-a-hoop honey cake. How delicious it smelled! Scrimshaw stopped playing his electric guitar, and Sweeney stopped howling.

Mrs. Oberon gave her grandson a huge slice of cake. His sore gums were soothed. His sadness was sweetened. He sighed with happiness, and sank into a soft, smiling sleep. Scrimshaw sighed with happiness, too.

"I'm worn out," he said, and collapsing into a chair, he turned on the television.

"Now, Scrimshaw," his mother cried, "turn off that television and come into the kitchen with me. I am going to show you how to bake cock-a-hoop honey cake yourself."

"But I don't have any blue borage honey in the house," cried Scrimshaw quickly. He knew that if he were taught to make cock-a-hoop honey cake, he might have to bake his own forever after.

"Never fear, my darling. I brought an extra pot of borage honey with me," said Mrs. Oberon with a big smile.

"You think of everything, Mum," cried Scrimshaw, getting out the eggbeater.

So Mrs. Oberon taught him how to bake his own cock-a-hoop honey cake, and when the cake was finished she said, "Very good. But now I must go home. Friends are depending on me."

So she went all the way home by skateboard, plane, raft, and trail bike. Vultures and alligators pretended not to see her going by.

And as she vaulted off the trail bike, her cats ran eagerly to meet her. "It's been a long day," said Mrs. Oberon, pouring milk into seven saucers.